OHIO DOMINICAN COLLEGE LIBRARY
COLUMBUS, OHIO 43219

Rosebud

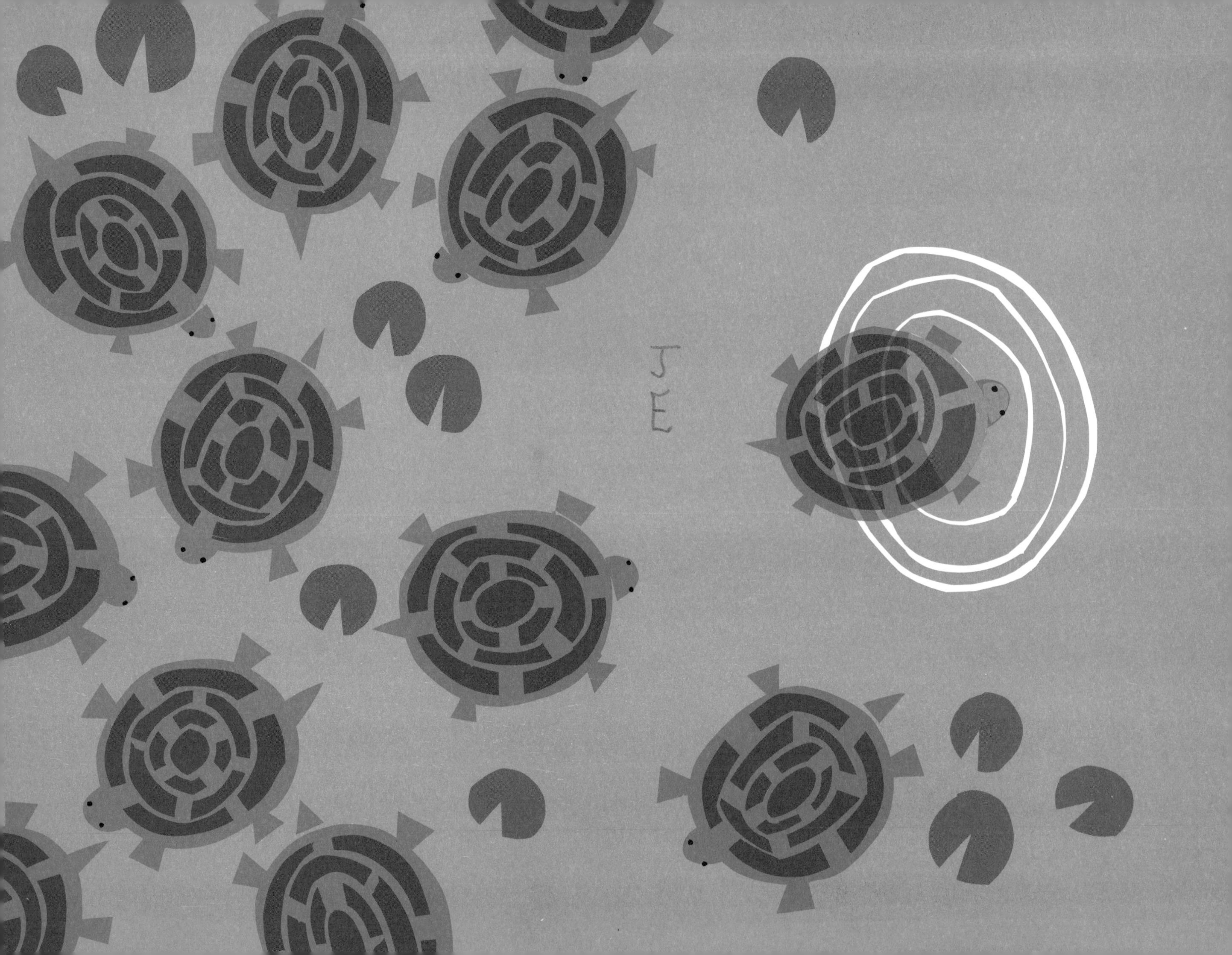

J
E

WRITTEN AND ILLUSTRATED BY ED EMBERLEY

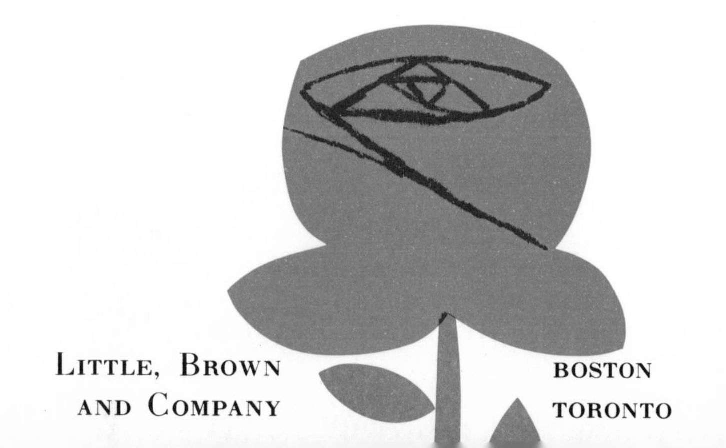

Little, Brown and Company

Boston Toronto

71560

Once upon a time there was a plain, ordinary little turtle who lived with a lot of other plain, ordinary little turtles on the edge of a muddy, murky little pond. Most of the little turtles were happy being plain and ordinary, and living on the edge of a muddy, murky little pond. But our little turtle was not. She was tired of being plain and ordinary and did not like living on the edge of a muddy, murky little pond.

COPYRIGHT © 1966 BY ED EMBERLEY. ALL RIGHTS RESERVED. NO PART OF THIS BOOK MAY BE REPRODUCED IN ANY FORM WITHOUT PERMISSION IN WRITING FROM THE PUBLISHER.
LIBRARY OF CONGRESS CATALOG CARD NO. 66–11006
Published simultaneously in Canada by Little, Brown & Company (Canada) Limited FIRST EDITION
PRINTED IN THE UNITED STATES OF AMERICA

One day as the little turtle sat watching the furry creatures come out of the tall green grass and go down to the edge of the muddy, murky little pond to drink, she thought to herself, "I would like to be a furry creature and go live in the tall green grass."

So that smart little turtle burrowed into the mud to get her back good and sticky. Then she crawled around among the pieces of fur and fuzz dropped by the furry creatures until her back was covered, a piece of lion fuzz here, a piece of zebra fur there. And when she no longer looked like a little turtle but looked instead like a furry creature, with a smooth green head, she went up to live in the tall green grass.

On the way to the tall green grass she passed a band of baboons sunning themselves on the smooth gray stones. Now you should know and I will tell you that it takes *very* little to make baboons angry. So, when they looked at the furry creature and it looked strange, smelled it and it smelled strange . . .

. . . they became *very* angry. They jumped, they jabbered, they jibbered, they hopped around, foamed at the mouth, rolled on the ground, threw things at each other . . .

. . . and finally one of them threw the frightened little turtle back out into the middle of the muddy, murky little pond.

The water washed the mud, fur and fuzz off her back, and she was glad of that. An old turtle she met in the middle on the bottom of the muddy, murky little pond told her that in all *his* one hundred and sixty-seven years all the turtles *he* had ever known were plain and ordinary and lived on the edge of the muddy, murky little pond.

But the little turtle did not give up. She remembered the beautiful feathered creatures that lived in the cool green trees on the edge of the muddy, murky little pond and thought to herself, "I would like to be a beautiful feathered creature and live in the cool green trees." So that clever little turtle burrowed into the mud to get her back good and sticky, then crawled around among the feathers dropped by the beautiful feathered creatures until her back was covered, a blue feather here, a red feather there. And when she no longer looked like a little turtle but instead looked like a little feathered creature she went up to live in the cool green trees.

She climbed out to the end of the branch and might have lived there awhile if . . . she had not tried to *sing*. Well, as you probably know, turtles *do not sing*, they HISS. And feathered creatures do not like hissing. It reminds them of snakes. So when the feathered creatures heard the hissing, they flapped they fluttered, they twittered they tweeted, they picked they pecked . . .

. . . and finally a large red feathered creature grabbed her and flew off into the sky hoping to drop the strange feathered creature onto the smooth gray stones. Luckily some feathers on her back came loose and the frightened little turtle dropped back into the middle of the muddy, murky little pond. This time she did not meet the old turtle, and she was just as glad.

After that the little turtle spent a lot of time in her shell, for she still did not like being plain and ordinary and she still did not like living on the edge of a muddy, murky little pond.

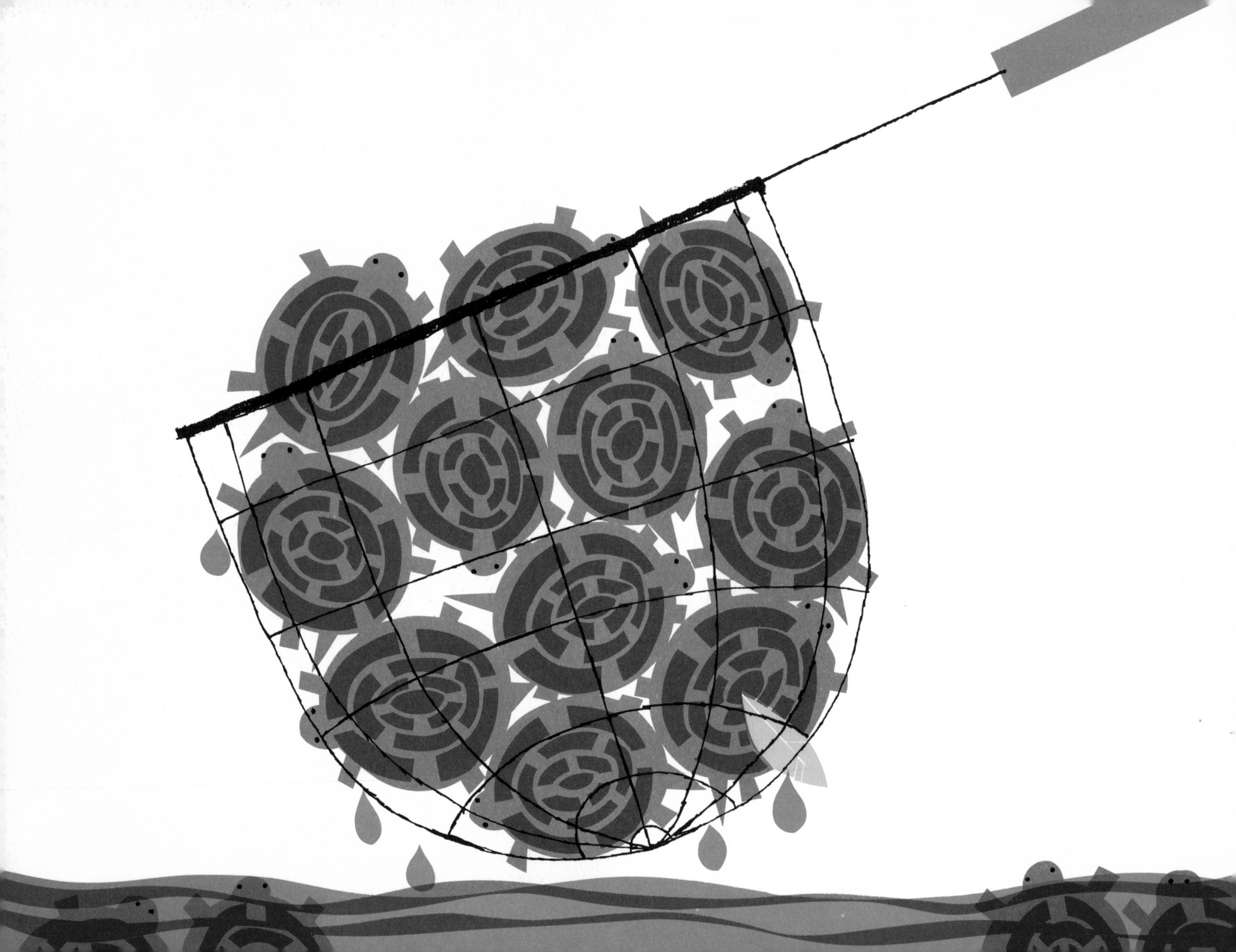

Then one day a large net came, scooped up our little turtle along with a lot of other plain ordinary little turtles and dropped them into a big black box.

Before our little turtle had a chance to be frightened she was taken from the box, scrubbed shiny clean and washed in fresh clean water—my that felt good—and she had a flower painted on her back.

She was put into a pan with the rest of her muddy, murky little pond friends who had been scrubbed, washed and flowered also. On Wednesday afternoon at three o'clock a small net came, scooped up our little turtle and dropped her into a small white box, which took her to her new home.

It was round and white, decorated with pretty little flowers, filled with white pebbles and cool clear water. There was a boat to play with, a castle to sleep in and a cool green lettuce leaf every day for lunch . . . The little turtle was very very pleased.

Because of the rosebud on her back, she was called Rosebud. And she lived happily ever after.